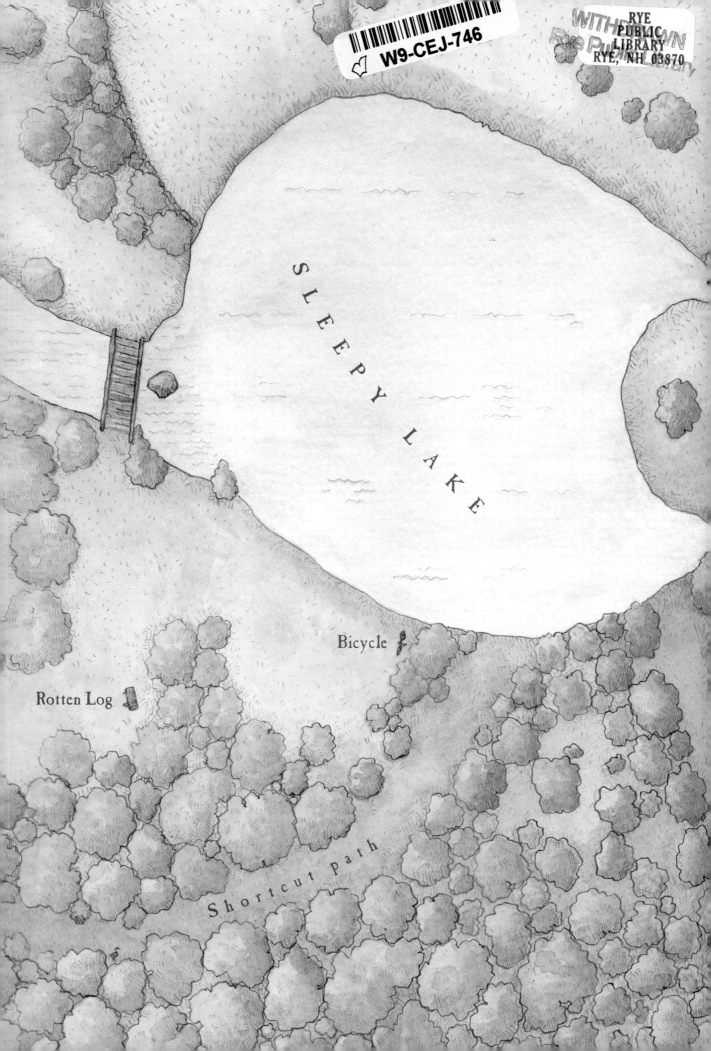

S L E E P Y   L A K E

Bicycle

Rotten Log

Shortcut path

# Absolutely Not

## Matthew McElligott

Walker & Company
New York

# For Christy

· · · · ·

First published in the United States of America in 2004
by Walker Publishing Company, Inc.

Published simultaneously in Canada by
Fitzhenry and Whiteside, Markham, Ontario L3R 4T8

For information about permission to reproduce selections from this book, write to
Permissions, Walker & Company, 104 Fifth Avenue, New York, New York 10011

Library of Congress Cataloging-in-Publication Data
McElligott, Matthew.
Absolutely not / Matthew McElligott.—1st ed.
p. cm.
Summary: Gloria, an ant, takes her friend Frieda on a walk and tries
to persuade her not to see danger in everything around her.
ISBN 0-8027-8888-2 (HC)  — ISBN 0-8027-8889-0 (RE)
[1. Friendship—Fiction. 2. Worry—Fiction. 3. Ants—Fiction.] I. Title.
PZ7.M478448Ab 2004
[E]—dc21                    2003047959

The artist used a combination of pencil, watercolor, and digital techniques
to create the illustrations for this book.

Book design by Victoria Allen

Visit Walker & Company's Web site at www.walkeryoungreaders.com

Printed in Hong Kong

2 4 6 8 10 9 7 5 3

· · · · · · · · · · · · · · · · · · · · · · · ·

$G$loria looked out the window. Summer was nearly over, and the first hint of fall was in the air.

"I have an idea," she said to her best friend, Frieda, "let's go for a walk."

"Absolutely not," said Frieda.

"But it's a beautiful day," said Gloria.

"Don't you want to get out of the house?"

"Absolutely not," said Frieda.

"You are a bug," said Gloria, "who is as
stubborn as a mule. Honestly, what are you
afraid of?"

"Well, for one thing," said Frieda, "I am
afraid of the snake."

"What snake?" asked Gloria.

"That one," said Frieda.

Gloria looked. She couldn't see a snake anywhere. "Do you mean the river?"

"What river?" asked Frieda.

"Put on your glasses," said Gloria, "and follow me."

Outside, the day was warm. The sky was bright blue and the air smelled of flowers. Gloria took a deep breath.

"Look around you," she said. "Isn't this a perfect morning?"

"Absolutely not," said Frieda. "It's frightening."

"Frightening?" said Gloria. "Why?"

"I'm not sure," said Frieda, "but I feel
like someone is watching us. I don't like it."

"Such imagination!" said Gloria.

Soon the bugs came upon an old, rotten
log lying in the grass.

"It's beautiful!" cried Gloria. "It stinks, and
it's covered in mold. Wouldn't it be lovely to
live here?"

"Absolutely not," said Frieda.

"Why not?" said Gloria. "Don't you like logs?"

"Did you say *log* or *dog*?" asked Frieda.

"Log," said Gloria. "L-O-G."

"Well, that's different then," said Frieda.

"You know what would be fun?" said Gloria. "Let's jump off
the log into that pile of leaves."

"Absolutely not," said Frieda. "It's full of frogs. They'll have
us for lunch!"

"There are no frogs," said Gloria. "It's just your imagination.
You find something bad in everything you see."

"That's not true," said Frieda.

"It *is* true," said Gloria. "To you, all the world looks dark and sinister."

Soon the bugs came to a clearing.

"A bicycle!" said Gloria.

"A giant!" said Frieda.

"A what?" said Gloria.

"Never mind," said Frieda.

"I've always wanted to ride one of these," said Gloria. "Shall we give it a try?"

"Absolutely not," said Frieda. "What if the owner comes back?"

"I'm sure the owner is far away," said Gloria.

"What if she's not?" asked Frieda. "Maybe she's just resting nearby."

"Look at me!" shouted Gloria. "What
fun! I'm riding a bicycle!"

"I think we should probably go home,"
said Frieda.

"I suppose you're right," said Gloria. "It is getting late. Let's take the shortcut through the woods."

"Are you sure that's a good idea?" said Frieda. "It looks like— "

"Have I been wrong so far?" asked Gloria.

"No, you haven't," admitted Frieda.

"You have to agree," said Gloria, "this really has been a nice day."

"I suppose it has," said Frieda. "Perhaps I worry too much."

"You really do," said Gloria.

"I can't help it," said Frieda. "It's just that sometimes things remind me of other things. For instance, those trees over there—"

"Oh, Frieda," said Gloria, "we've had a wonderful walk. Please don't ruin what's left of it."

"Very well," said Frieda, "But still—"

"But nothing," said Gloria.

"But Gloria," insisted Frieda, "doesn't it remind you of—"

"I'm not listening," said Gloria.

"Gloria!" shouted Frieda. "This time I'm sure! It really . . . is . . . a . . ."

"Oh, Frieda!" cried Gloria, "we were nearly dinner!"

Frieda shrugged. "These things happen."

"I should have been more careful," said Gloria. "How can I ever make it up to you?"

Frieda thought for a moment. "Well,"
she said finally, "there is one thing . . ."

"Anything," said Gloria. "Just name it."

"You could take me for another walk
tomorrow."

"Really?" said Gloria.

"Absolutely," said Frieda.

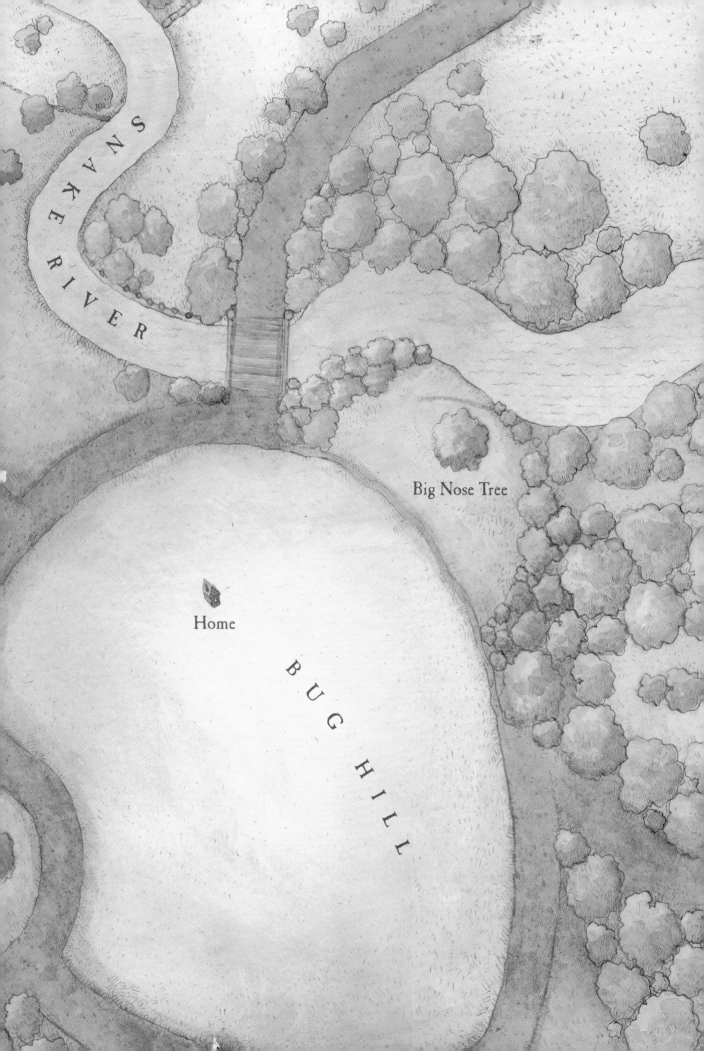

SNAKE RIVER

Big Nose Tree

Home

BUG HILL